NICK JR The BACKYARDIGANS
Mission To Mars

adapted by Wendy Wax
based on the original teleplay by Robert Scull
illustrated by Warner McGee

SIMON SPOTLIGHT/NICK JR.
New York   London   Toronto   Sydney

visit us at www.abdopublishing.com

Reinforced library bound edition published in 2007 by Spotlight, a division of ABDO Publishing Group, Edina, Minnesota. Published by agreement with Simon Spotlight, Simon & Schuster Children's Publishing Division.
Text by Wendy Wax based on the original teleplay by Robert Scull.
Illustrations by Warner McGee. Based on the TV series *Nick Jr. The Backyardigans*™ as seen on Nick Jr.®
Reprinted with permission of Simon Spotlight, Simon & Schuster Children's Publishing Division. All rights reserved.

 Simon Spotlight

An Imprint of Simon & Schuster Children's Publishing Division
1230 Avenue of the Americas, New York, New York 10020

Library of Congress Cataloging-In-Publication Data

This title was previously cataloged with the following information:
Wax, Wendy
    Mission to Mars / by Wendy Wax ; illustrated by Warner McGee
        p. cm. (The Backyardigans ; bk.#4)
    ISBN 978-1-4169-1486-0 (paperback)
    I. McGee, Warner, ill. II. Title. III. Series.
    [E]--dc22

ISBN-13: 978-1-59961-157-0 (reinforced library bound edition)
ISBN-10: 1-59961-157-0 (reinforced library bound edition)

All Spotlight books are reinforced library binding and
manufactured in the United States of America.

Uniqua, Pablo, and Austin were in the backyard.
"I'm Mission Commander Uniqua!" said Uniqua. "I'm getting ready to lift off on a mission to Mars."
"I'm the astronaut in charge of science!" said Pablo.
"I'm in charge of all the equipment we're bringing with us," said Austin.

"Mission Control here," Tyrone said to the astronauts. "We've been getting a strange signal from Mars. It goes: *'Boinga, boinga, boinga!'*"

"Space shuttle crew, we need you to find out what's making that noise," said Tasha.

"Affirmative!" said Commander Uniqua.

"Good luck, astronauts," said Tyrone. "We'll communicate with you from Earth."

"Roger that, Mission Control. Space shuttle ready for liftoff!" reported Commander Uniqua.

Tyrone counted down. "Five . . . four . . . three . . . two . . . one! Lift off to Mars!"

Up, up, up went the space shuttle, past the moon and around the stars.

"I see Mars!" cried Pablo.

"It's really red!" said Commander Uniqua. "Mission Control, we're approaching Mars and ready for landing!"

ol.

ustin called into the space shuttle.
wheeled vehicle with a robotic arm, appeared. He
ith important supplies.
ipment, we're ready for anything," said Austin.

"Congratulations,
"You're the first ast

"Here, boy!" A
R.O.V.E.R., a six-
was loaded down w
"With all this equ

"Here, boy!" Austin called into the space shuttle.

R.O.V.E.R., a six-wheeled vehicle with a robotic arm, appeared. He was loaded down with important supplies.

"With all this equipment, we're ready for anything," said Austin.

"Congratulations, shuttle crew!" said Tasha from Mission Control.
"You're the first astronauts to go to Mars!"

"Listen, Commander!" said Tasha from Mission Control. "We're getting that signal again!"

Boinga, boinga, boinga! came over the two-way radio.

"Find out where the noise is coming from, shuttle crew," said Tyrone.

"Roger!" said Commander Uniqua. They climbed aboard R.O.V.E.R. and set off.

"Look out!" cried Pablo. "It's a meteor shower!"

"It's a good thing we're ready for anything," said Austin. He pressed a button and a space umbrella popped out of R.O.V.E.R.'s trunk. The meteors bounced right off the space umbrella!

"We're having a small meteor shower," Uniqua reported to Mission Control.

Suddenly giant meteors started to fall around the astronauts.

"Shuttle crew, seek shelter at once!" ordered Tyrone. "I repeat: Seek shelter!"

The astronauts ducked into a cave and found themselves on the edge of a cliff.

"I wonder how far down it goes," said Commander Uniqua.

"It's a long way down," said Pablo.

"Then let's head back," said Commander Uniqua. "We don't want to lose contact with Mission Control."

But before they could go anywhere, the ledge cracked and broke off. "*AHHH!*" cried Commander Uniqua, Pablo, and Austin as they tumbled down into darkness.

Down, down, down went the astronauts. Finally they landed with a splash in an underground lake.

"We lost R.O.V.E.R.!" cried Austin.

"We'll find him, Austin," said Commander Uniqua. "We're ready for anything, remember?" Then she tried to call Mission Control. All she got was static.

Meanwhile, Tyrone and Tasha were getting static too.
"Our astronauts are lost forever on Mars!" Tyrone said sadly.
"But they're ready for anything!" Tasha reminded him.

"We're on a mission!" Commander Uniqua reminded her fellow astronauts. "Astronauts never give up. Follow me."

They began hopping from rock to rock—until there were no more rocks.

"Now what do we do?" asked Pablo.

Suddenly they saw a trail of bubbles in the water.

"What is *that*?" Austin asked.
Just then R.O.V.E.R. popped out of the water!
"R.O.V.E.R.!" shouted Austin. "You can swim!" The astronauts climbed aboard and headed toward the distant shore.

On the shore was an underground city.

"Martians live here!" said Commander Uniqua. "Let's take a closer look."

The astronauts left R.O.V.E.R. and climbed up a stairway that led to a house.

They rang the doorbell. A little martian opened the door!

"*Boinga!*" the martian said with a giggle.

"'*Boinga*' must mean 'hello'!" Austin said with excitement. They followed the little martian inside.

The martian picked up the phone and dialed a number. Then she handed the phone to Commander Uniqua. The martian had called Tyrone at Mission Control!

"Tyrone!" shouted Commander Uniqua. "We found out what's making that sound! It's a martian, and she's been calling you this whole time."

"Amazing!" said Tyrone. "What's her name?"

"What's your name?" Commander Uniqua asked the little martian.

"*Boinga!*" replied the little martian.

"My name is Uniqua," said Commander Uniqua.

"*Boinga*, Uniqua!" said the little martian.

"You sure say '*boinga*' a lot," said Pablo.

"We say '*boinga*' for almost everything!" said the little martian.

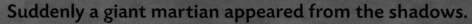

Suddenly a giant martian appeared from the shadows.
"*Boinga,* Mommy!" said the little martian.
"*Boinga,* honey," said the mommy martian. "*Boinga,* earthlings. I'm afraid we have to go to bed. But please come back any time."

"We will!" said Uniqua.
Then Uniqua picked up the phone and spoke to Mission Control.
"Mission accomplished!" Uniqua announced. "What's next?"
"Return to Earth!" said Tasha. "It's time for a snack!"

Austin, Uniqua, and Pablo met up with Tyrone and Tasha in the backyard.

"That was a very martian-y adventure," said Tyrone.

"It sure was!" said Uniqua. "*Boinga, boinga, boinga!*"

"*Boinga, boinga, boinga!*" shouted the others as they ran inside for a snack.